HENRY AND MUDGE

and the Forever Sea

The Sixth Book of Their Adventures

Story by Cynthia Rylant
Pictures by Suçie Stevenson

To Cheryl and Marc—CR
For Walker—SS

Henry and Mudge and the Forever Sea

Text copyright © 1989 by Cynthia Rylant
Illustrations copyright © 1989 by Suçie Stevenson

Published by arrangement with Atheneum Books For Young Readers,
An lmprint of Simon & Schuster Children's Publishing Division.

ISBN 978-1-942791-46-1 14740

Longtail Books
http://www.LongtailBooks.co.kr

Contents

To the Beach   5

The Forever Sea   13

Brave Dog   27

Good-bye, Crab   39

To the Beach

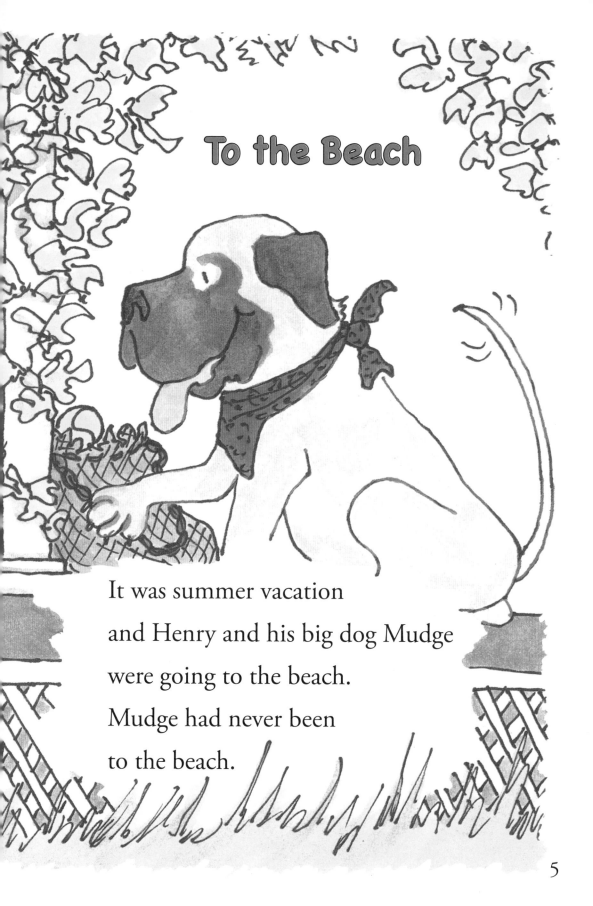

It was summer vacation
and Henry and his big dog Mudge
were going to the beach.
Mudge had never been
to the beach.

Henry promised
he would like it.
"You'll like the waves,"
he said.
"And the sand castles.
And the shells.
But don't drink the water!"
he warned.
"Too salty!"

They went in the car
with Henry's father.
In Henry's bag were
green goggles,
a yellow bucket,
an orange shovel,
and a dump truck.

In Mudge's bag were

a blue bowl,

a jug of water,

half of a bone,

and a tennis ball.

In Henry's father's bag were

a book about shells,

six towels,

and a red rubber lobster

he liked

to bring along.

They sang sea songs
all the way.
Henry's father said
"Yo-ho-ho"
about a hundred times.
Henry acted like a shark.
Mudge just wagged.
They couldn't wait
to get there.

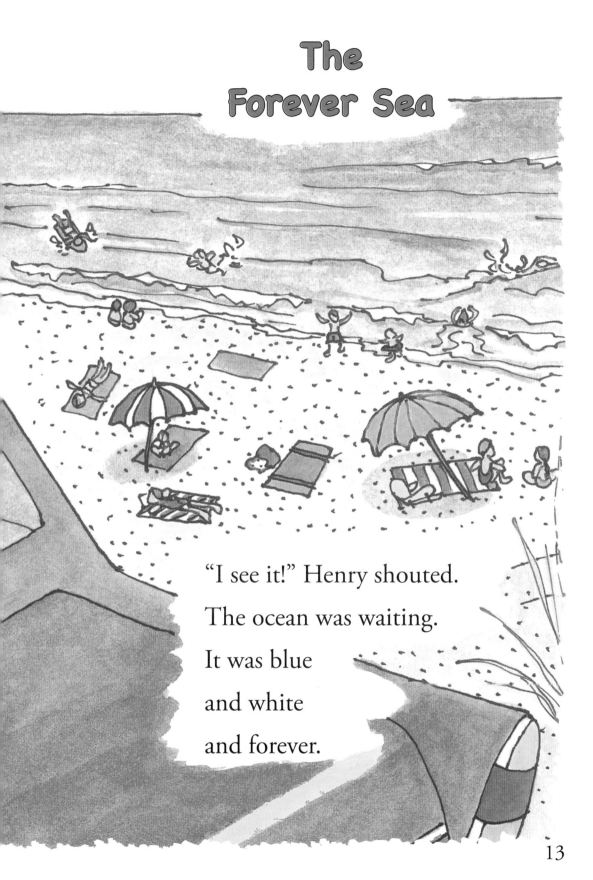

The Forever Sea

"I see it!" Henry shouted.

The ocean was waiting.

It was blue

and white

and forever.

Henry's father
honked the car horn.
Mudge barked.
They parked the car
and ran for the sand.

Mudge got there first.
He ran right into
the water.
SPLASH!

Henry was second.

SPLASH!

Henry's father was third.
SPLASH!

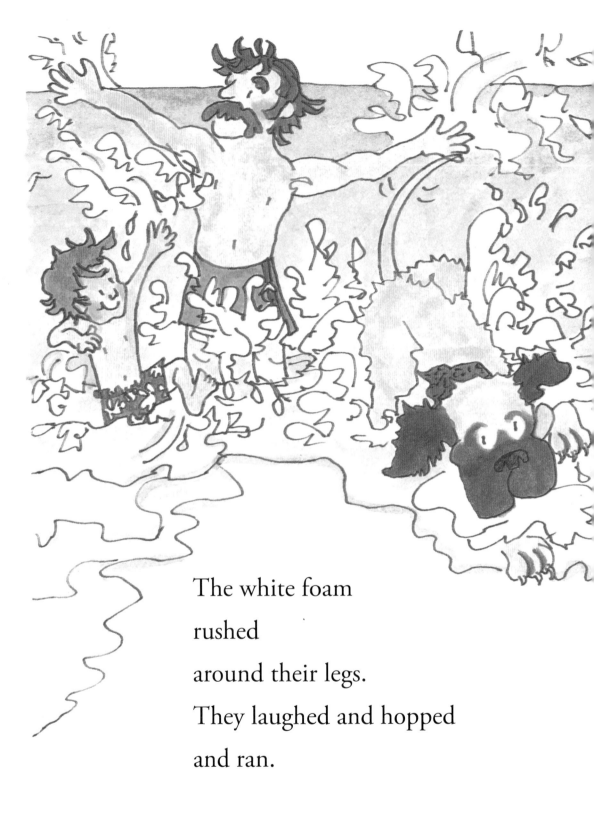

The white foam
rushed
around their legs.
They laughed and hopped
and ran.

A big wave
knocked Henry down.
He rolled
all the way
back to shore.

"Wow," said Henry.

He got up

and ran back in.

Henry's father
rode a wave
like he was
a surfboard.

21

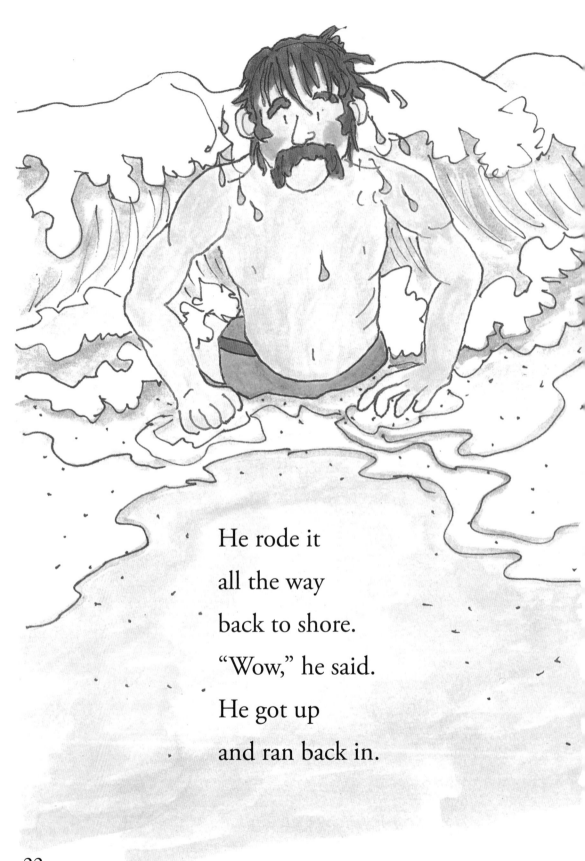

He rode it
all the way
back to shore.
"Wow," he said.
He got up
and ran back in.

Mudge was not as brave
as Henry and Henry's father.
He just ran
along the edge.
He stayed out
of the big waves.

But still he got
so wet
that he looked like
a whale with legs.

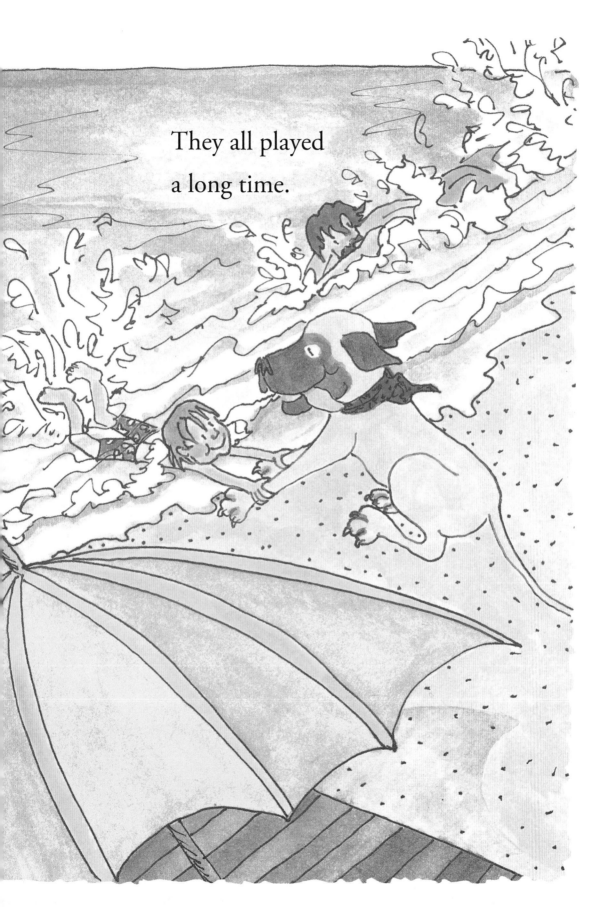

They all played
a long time.

Brave Dog

For lunch,
Henry and Mudge
and Henry's father
walked to a hot dog stand.

Henry had a hot dog
with ketchup.

Henry's father had a hot dog
with ketchup

and mustard

and onions

and slaw

and chili

and cheese.

"Yuck," said Henry.

Mudge had three hot dogs.

Plain.

In one gulp.

After lunch,
Henry and his father
began to build
a sand castle.

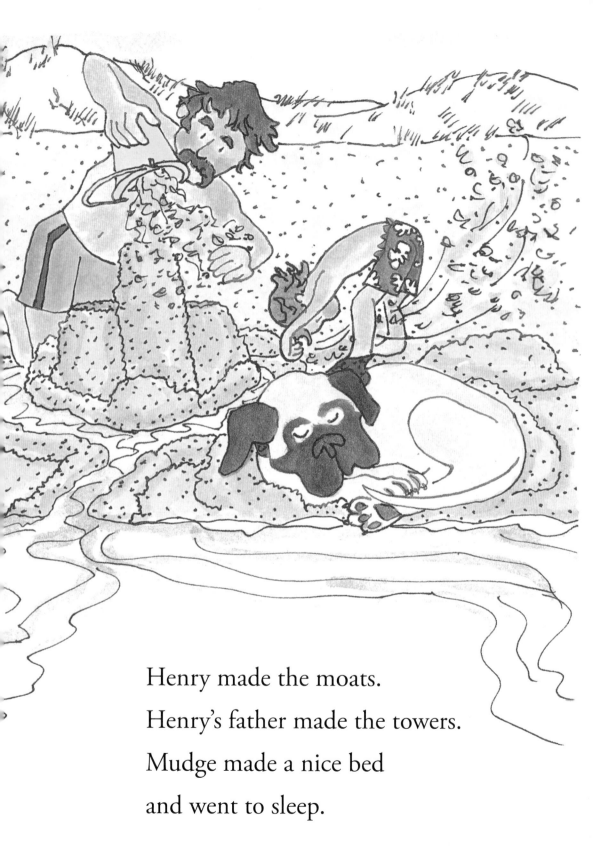

Henry made the moats.

Henry's father made the towers.

Mudge made a nice bed
and went to sleep.

When the castle was finished,
Henry's father
stuck his red rubber lobster
on the tallest tower.
Then he and Henry
clapped their hands.

Suddenly

a giant wave

washed far on the sand

and it covered everything.

It covered the moats.

It covered the towers.

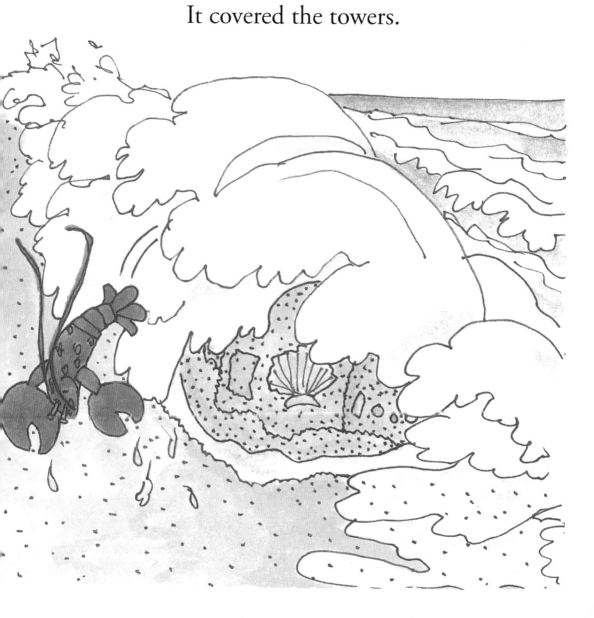

It covered Mudge, who woke up.

"Oops," said Henry.

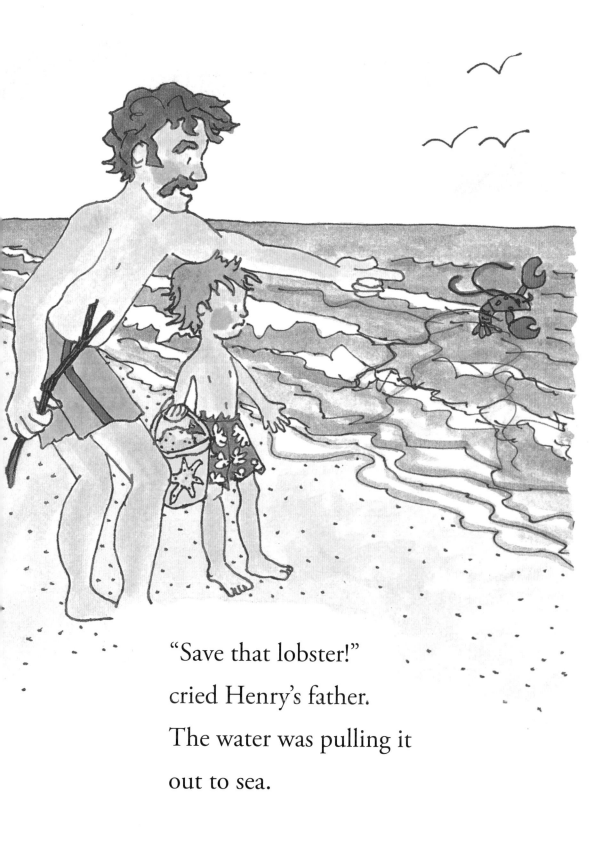

"Save that lobster!"
cried Henry's father.
The water was pulling it
out to sea.

Mudge ran and jumped
into the waves.
He caught the lobster
before it was lost forever.

"Good dog!" said Henry's father.
"Brave dog!" said Henry.
They all had cherry sno-cones
to celebrate.

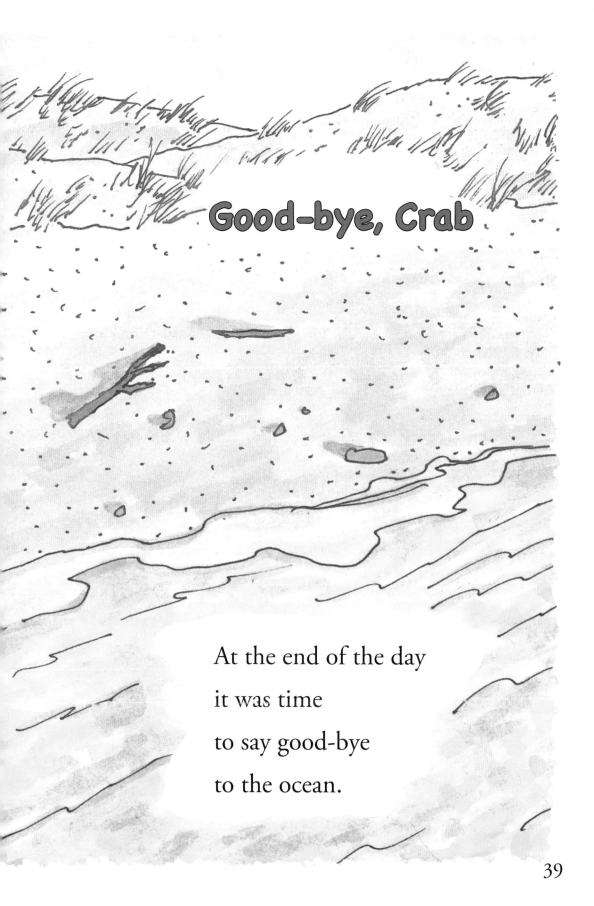

Good-bye, Crab

At the end of the day
it was time
to say good-bye
to the ocean.

Henry and Mudge
and Henry's father
walked along the sand,
watching the
orange sun set,
watching the
water sparkle
green and yellow.

Suddenly,
a crab popped out
from under the sand.
It came up sideways,
very fast.
So fast that Mudge
nearly stepped on it.

"Look out, Mudge!"
Henry said.
Mudge stopped
and put his nose
to the sand.
The crab looked at him.
He looked at the crab.

"I can't tell if that is
the front of the crab
or the back of the crab,"
said Henry's father.

Suddenly the crab ran,
sideways,
away from them.

Mudge chased it.
It popped back
under the sand.

Henry looked at its
new hole.

"Wow," he said.

"Wow," said his father.

Mudge stuck his nose
into the hole.
But nobody came out.

"Since we can't have
crab for dinner,"
said Henry's father,
"I guess we'll have
to have
another cherry sno-cone."

Henry cheered and hugged him.

As they walked down the sand,

Mudge stuck his nose

into every hole he saw.

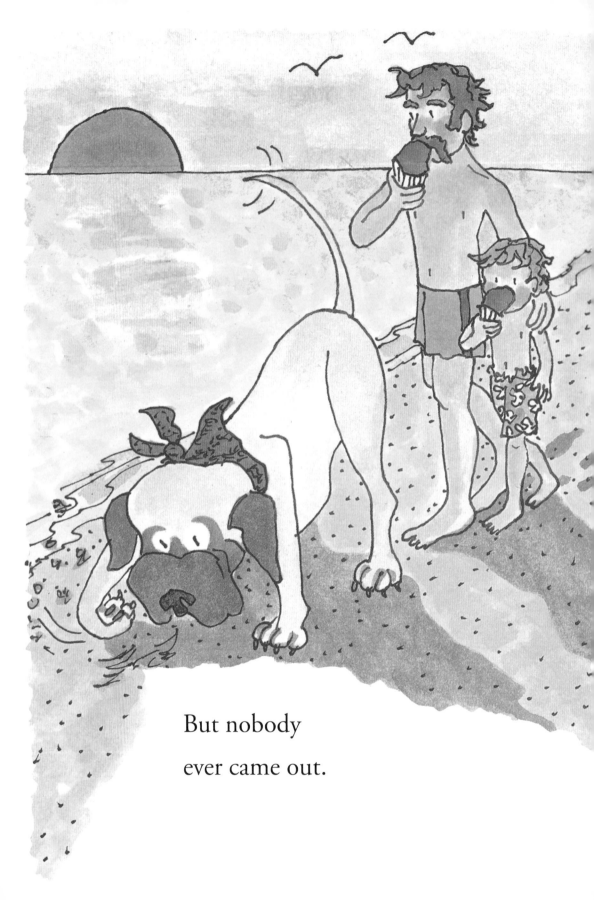

But nobody

ever came out.